BLUEE

in drag

poems by
TRACY RYAN

Bluebeard in Drag re-embodies the unsaid of our stories about family and memory. Tracy Ryan's poems examine the Gothic workings of power within the family, its incursions into the body, and how the body might resist, survive, and even heal.

Powerful, controlled and searingly honest, *Bluebeard in Drag* is compelling as an exploration of the resources of poetry, and as a human document.

Cover painting: Joy Hester (1920–1960 Australia), *Love* from the *Love* series, 1949–50, brush, ink, wash and pastel, 31.7 x 25.2 cm, National Gallery of Victoria.

Tracy Ryan was born and grew up in Western Australia. She has a Bachelor of Arts in Literature, and has also studied European languages at The University of Western Australia. She has worked in libraries, taught at Curtin University of Technology, and edited poetry and fiction for magazines.

Her first book of poetry, *Killing Delilah*, was published by Fremantle Arts Centre Press in 1994 and was shortlisted for the 1994 Western Australian Premier's Prize for Poetry and the John Bray Poetry Award, Adelaide Festival, 1996. She received a Category B Writer's Grant from the Literature Board of the Australia Council in 1996.

Photograph by Wendy Kinsella.

BLUEBEARD
in drag

POEMS BY
TRACY RYAN

FREMANTLE ARTS CENTRE PRESS

First published 1996 by
FREMANTLE ARTS CENTRE PRESS
193 South Terrace (PO Box 320), South Fremantle
Western Australia, 6162.

Consultant editor Wendy Jenkins.
Designed by John Douglass.
Production Coordinator Linda Martin.

Typeset by Fremantle Arts Centre Press
and printed on 110gsm challenge offset by PK Print, Western Australia.

National Library of Australia
Cataloguing-in-publication data

Tracy Ryan, 1964– .
Bluebeard in Drag

ISBN 1 86368 134 5.
I. Title.
A821.3

For
Sean Daniel Ryan
1962-1981

Acknowledgements

Some of these poems have been published or accepted for publication in *Hermes, Imago, Island, Mirage, Northern Perspective, Sightings* (Folio, 1995), *Texture, The Western Word* and *Westerly*, and broadcast on RTRFM radio.

The Geoffrey H Hartman quote is from 'On Traumatic Knowledge and Literary Studies', *New Literary History*, 1995, 26: 537-563. The Alice Miller quotations are from *Thou Shalt Not Be Aware* (NAL/Dutton, 1991).

The State of Western Australia has made an investment in this project through the Department for the Arts.

Publication of this title was assisted by the Commonwealth Government through the Australia Council, its arts funding and advisory body.

Contents

BLUEBEARD IN DRAG

*Every time we read we are in danger
of waking the dead, whose return
can be ghoulish as well as comforting.*

Geoffrey H Hartman

The victimization of children is nowhere forbidden; what is forbidden is to write about it.

...

The truth about our childhood is stored up in our body, and although we can repress it, we can never alter it ... someday the body will present its bill ...

Alice Miller

The Atonement

for Paul

Ever living beyond
his means he
pawned you
night after night to ease
this particular vice

thought
he couldn't lose

you'd always
be there
eyes raised like a
child saint

like altar wine the blood
turned his head he

thought
he was God thought
he couldn't lose

laid you out like
chips at blackjack

Twenty-one
You're gone

I stack
these words like
pennies too late
too late
to buy anything back.

Even by Day

These dreams arrive
like mail
wrongly addressed

I try
to send them back but
don't know their
origin

must have been meant
for an earlier tenant
one who's been driven
out

I cannot own
their content

always the same
the weight
coming down

like hand over
mouth
the rent
the pain

so real
I can smell him
taste his
sweat

Deposition

1

You ask me to state
exactly
what I remember
like some attendant
in theatre
relating incisions

Father, I was there but
somewhere near the ceiling
waiting to
come back in

2

I confess
I also loved you
does that jeopardise
my case

You sat me
on your knee, you
sang to me
passed on your fear like
a gift that had
cost you everything

At Mass you thrust me
under your arm like
a crutch

your grip crushed
my fingers
your whispers warm
with liquor, your pain
heavy as Jesus

Cyst

They pulled ten litres from me like
tapping a cask
no one would drink

all my body's
bellyaching
siphoned off like
excess fuel ripe
for a match

they'd never seen
such capacity

I lay
among tubes
proof of reconnection

my stomach
the world
after an earthquake &

me propped
like an ageing peevish God
still watching it all
go on without me.

Uniform

My mother was cut
vertically
her seamed belly
puckered
but tough
as the gabardine
she slashed
my uniform from

each piece pinned flat
to its pattern
held together by
an act of will or
imagination
one slip
one stitch awry
& you had
nothing to wear

Twenty years later
the method's more subtle
my own scar
horizontal braille for
lovers but otherwise
sealed
like lips the skin
resilient as lycra.

Wolf

A woman &
a redhooded girl
jostle
inside me
swallowed whole

I could plead
I was hungry
could say
she tempted me
but that's the lamest
story

Truth is, I don't remember how
these women got there

all I know is
one big bellyache
stretched
to bursting

I crave release
that first slice gaping
red satin

the skin
giving up
its ghosts.

Murder in the Dark

Reduced to
merely hearing
the whole skin becomes
an eardrum

sounding out
their argument —
advance, retreat

thought
this was a game
roles safely allotted

but everything's indistinct
by night

each scent
detached from
its parent

his beer breath
her sandalwood
perfume

child
drinks them in
like poison
can't tell
who's villain
who's victim.

Monster

I remember
that winter she took to bed
with glandular fever

he said
You look like death warmed up

his eyes flashed silver
as cheap condolences

his hands spanned
her neck, swollen, bolted,
but you're not sick
down there

her limbs spread
limp but
his need stitched her
together

over & over at night I
tried not to listen   willed her
to rise   to pursue him

but she only lay there
as I do now
possessed by the same fever
chasing that shape forever over the
glacier
that is my body, the white
waste spaces of the page.

Cycle

I am pressing these tiny tacks out
& into my body
securing freedom

sending the womb
messages like sweets
my mother told me never
to take from strangers

I am shelling the days neatly
as peas that will never reach
the table, I am

exercising control, choosing
carefully
my mistakes.

Orang-utans

1

The small gestures
trouble most
flick of a wrist as food's
picked over
bored stare matching us
behind glass

2

What do they do when
we're not watching:
give up the game
cease to exist
a solipsist's dream?

3

Once
the biggest hurled himself
at my daughter's image
four limbs splayed like
a car toy on glass
who knows what
he saw
It's the red hair
people joked but
she wasn't laughing

4

Now he swings like
a quoit round
the high pole
my daughter sings
I'm the king of the castle

5

Mother & child
hooked up like
tumbleweed

father
shuffling off on
hind legs

He walks like Frankenstein
my daughter says

& I correct
The monster.

Leeches

It wasn't so much the pain
swift and minor

it was the thought of the creature
battened on   sealed
like baby lips to nipple
unshiftable.

My brother would stride
into the murky creek
stir them up like
eye of newt or frog

take one end
& peel it back
limp as a sock.

I couldn't look
pictured the inside out
plush as a frayed nerve
my own veins cut up

he'd laugh
& turn them right again
still sucking.

Lesions

1

I pick at the past
like scabs   that are hard
as those barnacles   only visible
below the waterline

one summer diving
for the first time
I dashed my foot against those hundreds
of eyes clamped shut but sharp
as paper
surfaced like something
you couldn't keep
down

Hobbled for days, I watched
the red line rise
like mercury
to the groin.

2

You sealed off wounds
with your weird salve
like someone closing
debate

the hot wax
pooled cruelly and set
over any lesion
your obsession
perfectly airless.

Seal

Taken
for a siren
you give rise to
legend

the sailors
see only their desire
can't keep
away

Resistant
your layers
of fat like ermine you are
queen of
oblivion

even on ice your extremities
feel nothing

Swimming Lesson

Her small arms clap
round me like
the jaws-of-life

though once this
was her element
inside me

from me
she has learnt

mistrust
as a realist must learn
to mix colour

looks up at me
as a man
on the moon once
gazed at the earthrise

& had to believe
in getting back

My Daughter's Hair

Springs like blood but that
is the wrong red
its hot metal
precedes her like a warning
for the temperament
she's developed
out of hearing it
so often

I thought it was common & yet
so many remarks
from strangers
she wore her hat tight to put out
those tongues of flame.

Dominoes

Her father sent them
this year for Christmas
small slices of his past
and mine, rare constant
among passing high-tech toys.

I never knew
how to *play* them —
just slid them in and out of
their pallid coffin,
set them up to fall.

I delighted in
their pattern, intricate on
the back as the fancy
biscuits Mum served to visitors,
the other side secret
as code.

Now reading my daughter
the rules I find
it's all about calculation and
offloading, piece by piece —
the first one free
cries 'domino, I win'.

My daughter says
they look like thunderclouds.

Housewarming

Dampened only by dispute
over property lines

though the place
looks neat, defined,

the weeds
controlled, the whole
risen from rubble like

an ambition
unquestionable
upright

though here's
a cape lilac
shedding its deadly
bubbles.

Inside I sit
little match girl on
his polished oregon

the inlaws are nodding
the wife swelling like
pale berries

he harps on
the litigation
she tears at a piece of
half-charred meat

my visions dwindle on the
well-fed air.

Host

No sacrifice for him
steak after steak laid thick
as headstones on the hotplate

I step
between family tables
collate my platter
of meagre vegetables
cannot take part.
His juices permeate the lot

He says
Why don't you eat
his bite a sudden bloody
cross-section.

Hand-me-downs

They persist in photos
through the years
like a family
resemblance, like
the garments
of saints, or relics
of uncertain origin —
maybe some cousin
who pitied us
whose largesse
smothered us each in turn
with houndstooth wool
pulling at throat and wrist
visitations from
the world
of style
ten years too late but
our mother made
us over
a set of dolls
the same child forever and ever
shrinking to fit.

Bridal

Despatched, like so many crisp
white parcels
to anywhere

they're stripped now
of uniform
& each must find
her own way

all that's left
a video
that gets scratchier each year
though no one watches it

snapshots caught
at that point
between smile & rage

& those dresses in
cupboards intact
as a silkworm's sheath.

Handmade

My efforts were always holed
like a badly typeset page

Mum could splice but I
could only knot, the underside
lumpy as braille, the wearer
reading my faults

Stubborn, I knitted on
as if sharpening knives

refused the help which meant
her taking over —

a Frankenstein garment

I laboured alone, perfecting
tension, casting off

learning that code
my brothers scoffed at
because they coveted it

& the names, suggestive, female
stocking   garter   purl

The Silver Sheaffer

Recalls so many offices
from the wrong side of the
desk, its very weight
forcing decisions

the sort you get for your twenty-first
trying out styles:
all those versions of yourself you
signed away
next to his or his illegible script

the house you rented
scheduled for demolition
the child you duly registered
forms of consent to this
ward or that prescription

& then the men in suits
taking your statement:
how long apart & whether
intending to reconcile.

The World's Best Fairytales

These were the first lies
you gifted me
FROM MUMMY & DADDY, 1969

I could read then already
I remember the headline
MAN WALKS ON MOON

less real, less useful
than Andersen
memory flattening everything
to a page

Like an astronaut
on re-entry I
come back to this volume

so thick it could stand
by itself, as weighty
as Bible or dictionary

though spineless now &
yellowed, it's the one thing
that has survived
along with me.

Anonymous

At dawn
for a terrible moment
she forgets
whose leg it is that
closes over her, soft shackle,
whose hands
locked over her wrists & neck
last night, whose anonymous
body tried hers so gently over
& over that later
her thighs will twinge
like conscience
& she'll remember
only his face hooded
in the half-night.

Caveat

My skin beneath you is pink &
new as the skin
under a blister

tenuous, taking
any impression

You persist like
sunburn

whichever way I
turn I
cannot lie easily.

Fusion

Your blood with mine
like two thumbs
pressed together in childhood
the daughter between us a pulse
that won't give up
though we have tried to separate
delicately, as a surgeon separates twinned
babies, but even the organs
have merged, we compete
for food for speech half of me is lost
in your body.

Shower

Once we stood
here together, the air
white as if
on fire

until we couldn't see
each other

you soaped me
all over
losing your grip

steamed me
open.

The differences
seemed less then —
an illusion
of newness

of bodies so
fluid so
possible
nothing could
soil us.

Now I start the day
alone   the only cloud my
breath   baulk to think of
old extravagance
aware the heat
runs out.

Number One

This is a musty house
gritty as graves
a house
stopped in winter

awash in horns
from the harbour
stench of sheep ships & the oyster
supply opposite
here in the meaty city

Meant to remake it mine
never thought to knock on walls
porous as bone

damp invading stone
a film on the skin
sharp taste on tongue
stealing speech

Sticky bailiff
fingering lungs & soul
I should
wrench open windows
make fires & dance
myself rid of you.

Pride

I saw her tonight
swept along
in the parade
her head
newly shaved
under a black cap

she danced
with fists raised
at enemy lines

I thought
our eyes met
but she wouldn't
know me

face pale as the ghost
of a former self
dress inconspicuous
as all the wallflowers
lining William Street

so close I could have
touched her
just once

again

& she'd have felt
the power
go out.

Object Relations

1

Both soft & hard
like the sandalwood
whose scent blends
with her saltsweet

weightless as sandalwood she is
of untold value

found art I
don't know
how to treat how
to handle.

2

I'm dry as
paper   her constant
heat shows up
my acid secrets
weak as citrus but only too
legible.

3

I don't want her to go
in there that's
a closet of bodies & I'm
Bluebeard in drag or
Dracula just over
her shoulder these
undead
lead on my
ankles my
veins distended with
bad blood I
spread my hungers

don't want her
to be next.

4

Still we cling
two children to one
comforter   a rug
everything's
swept under.

Spring again, can I stand it

— Margaret Atwood

1   Gift

Soft from sun he reclines
on the spring lawn

I bring him
a small snail with shell
slight as a baby's
fingernail

watch it curl
the underside
so vulnerable

then suckle on
his skin

like wet
razor blades
he says
without wincing

2 Weather eye

This breath that blooms & glows
unexpectedly between
my breasts

the grassy sweetness
of his uncut
hair

the swelling the
opening all so much

more predictable than
any season

why then this
weather eye in the certain
dark

3   Reviving

He is coming at me like someone
reviving an argument
again & again as if by
sheer persistence
he could push through
me to somewhere
before logic

madness how hands mouths tongues can
so quickly reach an agreement
in spite of us

4   Impedimenta

He brings me
a lizard's tail
in an old
vodka bottle

it lies
like a dropped claw

tiny sword that
would have rusted
to nothing in the
October air

instead held
as evidence
of the uncaught

what rolls so light
in my hands altogether
too weighty
for the creature

& I wonder
how many times
can the lizard
do this

Learning to Read

Maybe the great poets were
wrong, maybe it's never unique

Celia/Julia/Beatrice
lovely variations but generic

maybe I miss
not his particular imprint

but simply
body against body

flat & archetypal as
the tarot cards

the course of it
predictable

patterns repeating like
wallpaper like

these vague pronouns
I could pin down

but he's not even
the first of that name

& maybe I say this
to all the boys

& this is the last of all
love poems.

Making Up

1

I said you are a good girl
I said I am not like you
(my head full of metal)

she hasn't worn
high heels
or make-up for years
I said
      I'd like to see
some colour in those cheeks
(sculpted and gently
feline)

let's go somewhere
outrageous and
you can dress up
she said
      I'd have to
do Jenny Craig I need to
lose ten pounds did you see
Paris is Burning *I'm not gay but I*
loved it

2

Imagine being
that close, fingering in
the foundation like
lotion or
massage oil

the tender half-moons under
each eye

the stroke of rouge along
the bone as if I
had laid my hand there

then painting in
the deep lips
kissing them skin-pink again

3

She's a found poem
I can't improve on
what I could say hangs in
the air like an insect she
brushes away

Near Miss

Nothing so usual
as that bus
that veered off-schedule
around the corner
& into the girl on her way to school

who was top of her class in two languages
before they shaved her
baby-bald & tottering
& she began again
spitting words like unfamiliar food

in that house her parents
had bought from us
when Dad went bankrupt
& we moved to another suburb

Later, the hair grew back
blacker, primeval.

Exegesis

Her body is a palimpsest   was it ever virgin   bears
words like wounds   in shorthand   scar   on the left
foot   running after her mother to the river   a whole
winter she can't remember   sealed in there   shoulders
riddled with freckles   a secret code the heat brings out
that summer   at Rockingham   with her father   who
denies it   who denies her   body   layers peel off like
drafts or depositions   truths gone underground   to
stomach or womb   irretrievable

Rous Head

Out on a land-limb
a stiff upper lip when seen
from above as on a map

night winks
its illegible
signals

red/green our
words pulse and
disappear.

Go on. No, you.
I shouldn't ask this.
But.

Extrapolate
project out here where
there's no looking
back

where wind nags from all possible
angles.

Generations

You are going soon
I try out each feeling like a ruse
a combination

your last gesture a holiday
back home
where the dumb cousins
don't want you

you are desperately seeding but
the roots don't take

neat bonsai we cannot
we cannot
little parodies of
your lusts your designs we
bend we distort
a portrait in
multiples
there may be more of us
we are voices in the head of your dead
schizophrenic brother your pretty
sister they
locked away because
she was beaten

We haunt the trees of your hometown
European green the emblem of invasion
where clothes steam bodiless
on the morning line
stiff as perfection

in this coldest of cities where
we all come home
crisscrossing the
continent like
generations of gossip
piecemeal a history
worn & blurred as these bluestone
cobbles under wastewater

At thirty you leave
snatching a child for luck
or spite
it sits among cinders, drinks watered-down milk
while you go to work
& pubs & dances
in quest of the next
stepmother

> *i become the child* i am eight
> i crouch in windows but never
> get out his shoulders shadow me
> unseen as in all melodramas
> i have no audience
> to warn me
> am taut & green as a
> string bean hide my legs
> from the boys
> i give up dancing
> i build castles of food in the rotten
> bottom drawer of my bedroom
> i secrete

sweets tell lies & go
skating bring
home twenty kids from school
to see the horse that doesn't
exist

In the house where no light enters
where my sister sits in the window of fear
drawing her words out of me
I patch & soften
corners with cobweb
pushed through
easy as gauze or
hymen
my spiderbelly swelling with a million
reproductions
you'll crush by stepping on

How can I be daughter mother wife
I'll shave
my head/collaborator
parade
our shame through streets
but the whole world
is Vichy

COVER YOUR EYES YOUR MOUTH

I give birth
to a bastard
between two languages I will tell it
I had to survive

i am the boy bent under the bed
at the sound of your step

     the wife whose cunt
     is never allowed to be sick

Kathleen bruised as a raincloud

     the first son dead
     of no one listening

the last son questioning
windows with fist & rock

At home   in this coldest of cities
your real name swears at you & you act
shocked.

Analysis

1   feeling

you
            are the elephant & I am
            five blind men feeling
            you up for sense & my ten
            hands all tell
            different stories

            are the jigsaw in the
            mad ward
            recreation room
            critical bits always
            missing but
            the wholeness anyway
            an illusion

            fill it in

            finally   it's still
            only a partial
            view   doing this says
            more about me than
you

2   regression

without moving
you break all my bones tell me
this is necessary
for resetting O excellently
smooth operator

unfolded am an
insect pinned here hardly
beautiful

will
shed & leave
nothing but shell

evolving backwards through
all kinds of animal
you do not mean
to kill but
your wordlessness is
surgical

3   accident / you

are my dead brother who
took everything apart
the antique clock
the chemicals
the minerals
the tv set he could always put
together again slick
technician
till one day something
went missing
& he had nothing
but a box
of noise

turned his glass on
the cat's tail
& burned it
                    an accident
unrepentant scientist
tinkering with his
lusts by
proxy
dismembering
me   maybe
the part you need
was never there

4　fall

however close we
get there are laws that
exclude collision don't
understand them want
some disaster cosmic not
this occasional syzygy
& attendant eclipse
am sick
of this imagery too
global precise want
a smaller scale
the folly of
Icarus the reek
of burning
feathers of hot
wax

5   echo's chamber

this is that box of noise
it goes
no further

pain rebounds here
a policy of
containment

she has
a very small voice
it's all that's left of her

she is willing
to reproduce
your silences

exactly

Vampyre

1 *Seven years, if you want to know*

Between visits the blood
is dull
unobtrusive

no one notices
the night-changes

Strangely hungry I
stiffen my collars &
dream

wrists let out red
before you I

take up your vices like a
complaint

feel for this pulse like an old
metre that has to
break *the last heave*

Something is rubbing off
unseen as skin cells

your pallor a screen
for projection

your mouth sure as the shrink
you both eat &
drink me you need me
to live

2　*If I've killed one man*
　　I've killed two

Is that
a bruise
on your neck

Change the subject I won't
bleed like that
on his slick
Stainmaster

The clock
marks each
expensive minute
someone's paying for

I pull at holes
in my old shirt
peel dead
skin from nails look
anywhere but at

him take words in both
hands & drive
home eyes shut

Memento

Whenever her sisters, superstitious,
threw out the little Buddha,
my mother carried it back.

Brought by her father
or grandfather from India,
sleek and androgynous,
the child-Buddha smiled
keeper of a secret.

First she dislodged it from
the cleft in a tree
then it beckoned from the garbage
one palm serene on knee
the other hand pointing

baffling everyone
with its insistent return.

It followed her into marriage
and her own seven children
who watched it darken
twenty-three years, unpolished,
greenish and smelling like money.

For 'David', Born Hillcrest, Probably 1960

All this time your birth like words
hidden in the fold of a page.

The details are faded, sporadic.
I keep my ear
to the ground for them, I am
forging your papers, hoping
you'll collect, but this is
underground and we
may never meet.

This is a cold, cold war, this is
your belated birthday party.
Blindfold, I fumble,
pin the name on the brother.

All my life I have stumbled over
you, persistent
bump in the family carpet,
air bubble in the Christmas
snowstorm ball I shook
and shook but couldn't fill.

You were as real
as insinuation
you crept in when voices dropped.

Glimpsed once in the dark
of our mother's eyes like a slide
stuck briefly in a projector,
you were everywhere but flimsy
as fingerprints.

I am gathering evidence.
I am scattering dust like a loved one's
ashes over thirty years of lies
and when I blow
I know I will find you.

She has folded them back
into her body
— Sylvia Plath

(A Poem in Eight Voices)

1

I wince when you say 'I have
six children', ignoring
me, stepmother to my Gretel

the trail
to my 'real' mother eaten away

2

You could have sung like
Piaf on corners
left me in hotel rooms
in my cot, you should have got what you
wanted no *little sparrow* but
a *pocket Venus* the Italian
tenor said

I know
this tale heard
through caul through womb
draw it out, the sticky web of our
connection

It is my own name
I cannot speak

Me or
your honour back then
not to mention money
I was breastfed for a week, went
to a good family.

3

The second-born
I replace him
presentation
to angry private gods

Your defiant
nunc dimittis

& I try fate, eat
poison, fall from trees
into thorns
with eyes unharmed
no small Oedipus

I outwit your oracle
escape like air at eighteen.

4

Little Louisa May you say who must
carry these stories no one else
will tell
Jo tiding the Marches
over lean times
with pen & paper
with shaven head

If I'd been a boy

you said & hid
your own name
between mine &
the one I inherited

a scapular
worn under everything

dying like this I'll be lifted
straight to heaven.

5

Break a few hearts that one
                              said
over the dimpled chin
you look for some resemblance but
I marry early   you

take me to the GP
for a pill I'm already on
how can I tell you

how can I ask you
what these looks mean?

6

Your spitting image
whose diary screams
Bitch
you ground me for weeks I
smoke   bleach
my hair to undo
our correspondence.

7

Want to
melt into you

8

Finish off the family
born on the same date
as the first &
always the last to leave
any party.